For Linus
V.C. and C.F.

Library of Congress
Cataloging-in-Publication Data Available

10 9 8 7 6 5 4 3 2 1

Published in 2001 by Sterling Publishing Company, Inc
387 Park Avenue South, New York, N.Y. 10016

First published in Great Britain in 2001 by David & Charles Children's Books, Winchester House,
259-269 Old Marylebone Road, London NW1 5XJ

Text © Vicki Churchill 2001
Illustration © Charles Fuge 2001

Distributed in Canada by Sterling Publishing
c/o Canadian Manda Group, One Atlantic Avenue, Suite 105
Toronto, Ontario, Canada M6K 3E7

Printed and bound in China

Sterling ISBN 1-4027-0023-7

Sometimes I Like to Curl up in a Ball

Written by Vicki Churchill
Illustrated by Charles Fuge

Sterling Publishing Co., Inc.
New York

Sometimes I like
to curl up in a ball,
So no one can see me
because I'm so small.

Sometimes I like to jump
high as I can,

To see how much
noise I can make
when I land.

Sometimes I like to just
walk round and round,

I pigeon step, pigeon step,
till I fall down.

Sometimes
I like to
stand
still as
a tree,

And watch
everyone
rush around
about me.

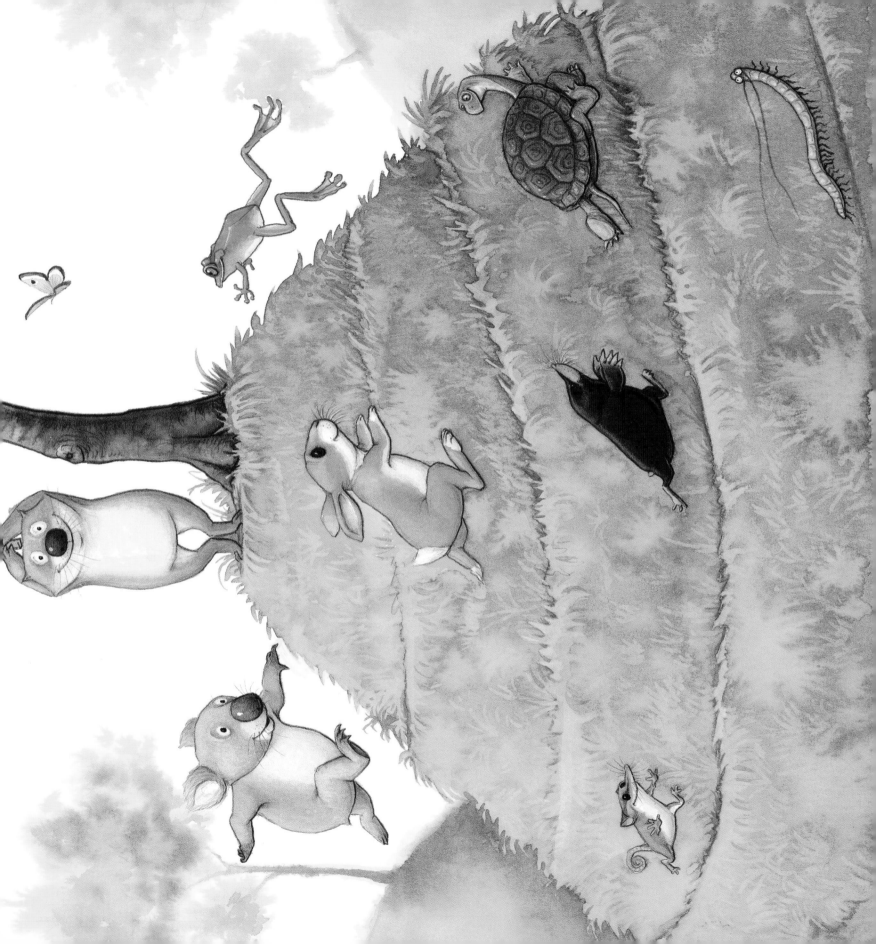

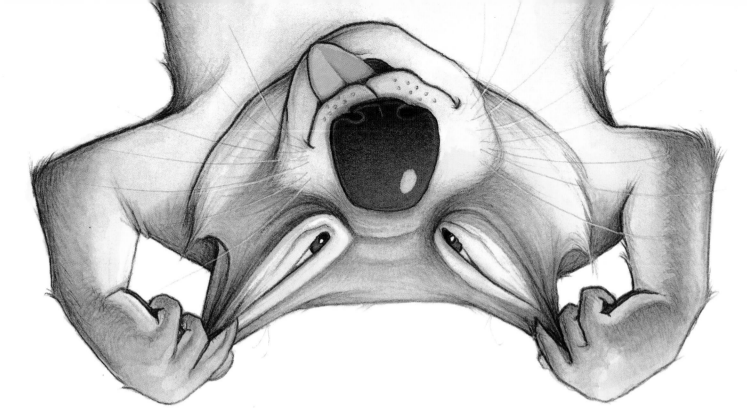

Sometimes I like to
poke out my tongue,

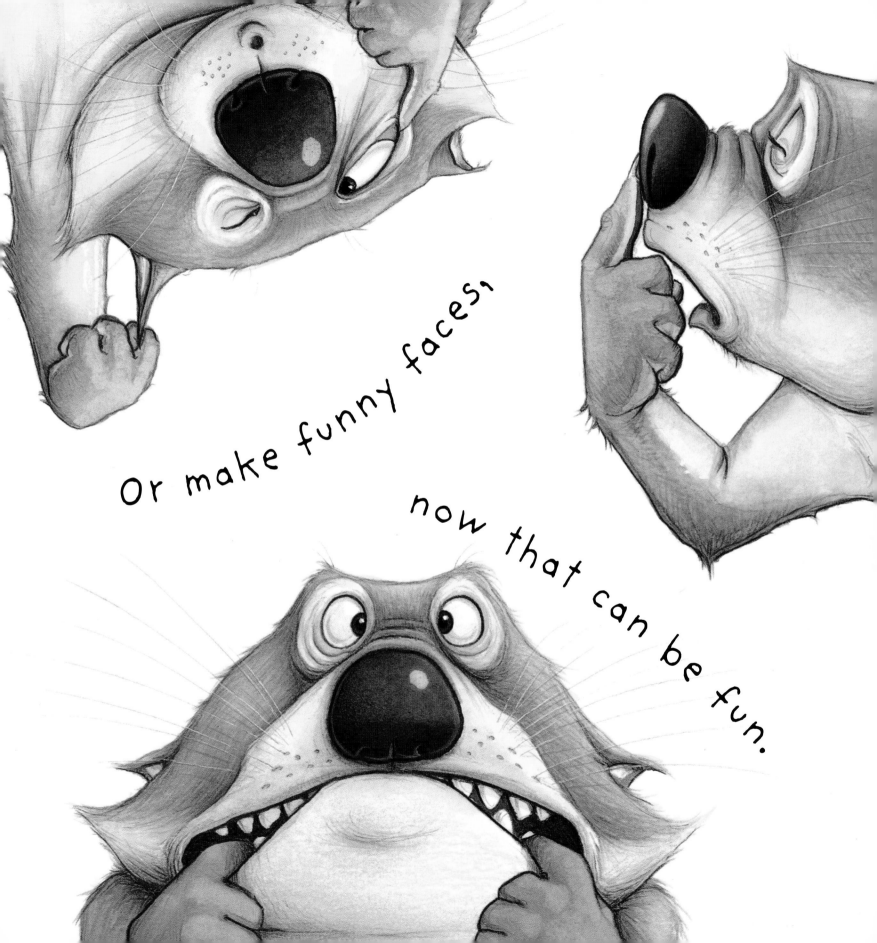

Or make funny faces, now that can be fun.

Sometimes I like to get
in a real mess,

With mud on my feet and
my hands and my chest.

Sometimes I like to run
ever so fast,

I sometimes come first,
but I sometimes come last.

But when the day ends
and the sun starts to fall,
Then I do what I do best of all.
I find somewhere soft,
somewhere cozy and small...